HANS CHRISTIAN ANDERSEN

Thumbelina

unabridged translation by Erik Haugaard
illustrated by ARLENE GRASTON

For TPC,
who is my very own
Thumbelina

and for Charlie,
who is my Everything

—A.G.

Published by Delacorte Press
Bantam Doubleday Dell Publishing Group, Inc.
1540 Broadway
New York, New York 10036

Doubleday and the portrayal of an anchor with a dolphin are trademarks of Bantam Doubleday Dell
Publishing Group, Inc.

Text copyright © 1974 by Erik Haugaard
Illustrations copyright © 1996 by Arlene Graston

Library of Congress Cataloging-in-Publication Data

Andersen, H. C. (Hans Christian), 1805–1875
[Tommelise. English]
Thumbelina / Hans Christian Andersen ; translated by Erik Haugaard ;
illustrated by Arlene Graston.
p.   cm.
Summary: After being kidnapped by an ugly toad, a beautiful girl no bigger than a thumb has a
series of dreadful experiences before meeting a fairy prince just her size.
ISBN 0-385-32251-8 (hc:alk. paper)
[1. Fairy tales.] I. Haugaard, Erik Christian. II. Graston, Arlene, ill. III. Title.
PZ8.A542Th 1997   95-53284
[E]—dc20   CIP
                                                                             AC

Manufactured in the United States of America
The text of this book is set in 14-point Garamond.
Interior design by Arlene Graston
Jacket design by Kimberly M. Adlerman

October 1997
10 9 8 7 6 5 4 3

*O*nce upon a time there was a woman whose only desirc was to have a tiny little child. Now she had no idea where she could get one, so she went to an old witch and asked her: "Please, could you tell me where I could get a tiny little child? I would so love to have one."

"That is not so difficult," said the witch. "Here is a grain of barley; it is not the kind that grows in the farmer's fields or that you can feed to the chickens. Plant it in a flowerpot and watch what happens."

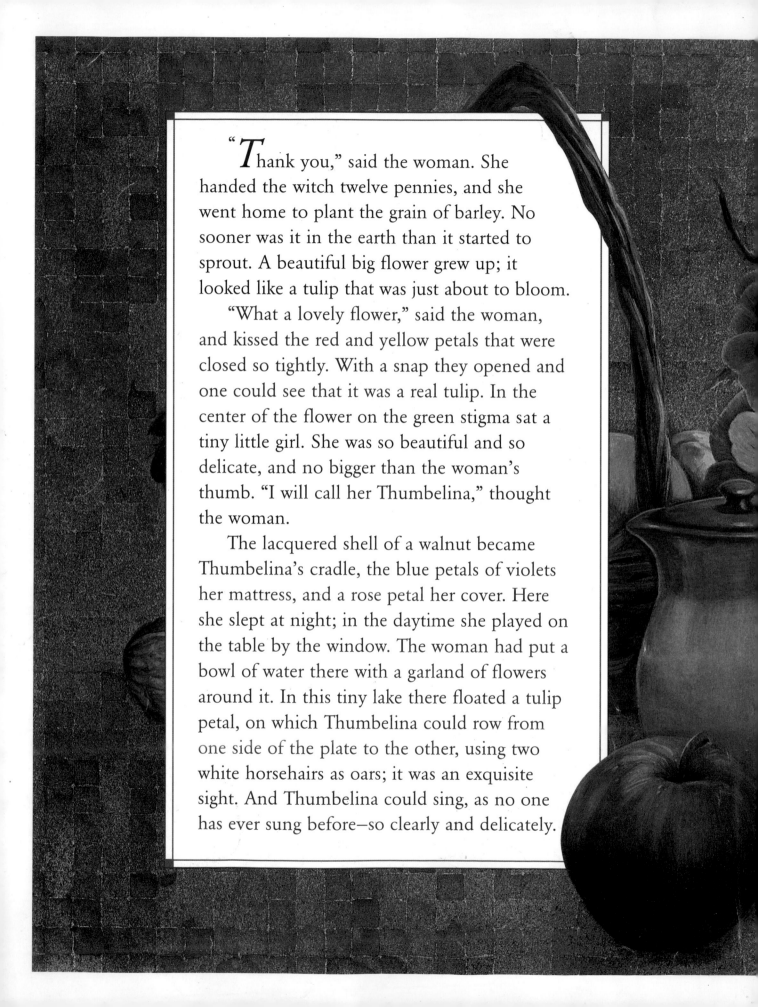

"*T*hank you," said the woman. She handed the witch twelve pennies, and she went home to plant the grain of barley. No sooner was it in the earth than it started to sprout. A beautiful big flower grew up; it looked like a tulip that was just about to bloom.

"What a lovely flower," said the woman, and kissed the red and yellow petals that were closed so tightly. With a snap they opened and one could see that it was a real tulip. In the center of the flower on the green stigma sat a tiny little girl. She was so beautiful and so delicate, and no bigger than the woman's thumb. "I will call her Thumbelina," thought the woman.

The lacquered shell of a walnut became Thumbelina's cradle, the blue petals of violets her mattress, and a rose petal her cover. Here she slept at night; in the daytime she played on the table by the window. The woman had put a bowl of water there with a garland of flowers around it. In this tiny lake there floated a tulip petal, on which Thumbelina could row from one side of the plate to the other, using two white horsehairs as oars; it was an exquisite sight. And Thumbelina could sing, as no one has ever sung before—so clearly and delicately.

*O*ne night as she lay sleeping in her beautiful little bed, a toad came into the room through a broken windowpane. The toad was big and wet and ugly; she jumped down upon the table where Thumbelina was sleeping under her red rose petal.

"She would make a lovely wife for my son," said the toad; and grabbing the walnut shell in which Thumbelina slept, she leaped through the broken window and down into the garden.

On the banks of a broad stream, just where it was muddiest, lived the toad with her son. He had taken after his mother and was very ugly. "Croak . . . Croak . . . Croak!" was all he said when he saw the beautiful little girl in the walnut shell.

"Don't talk so loud or you will wake her," scolded the mother. "She could run away and we wouldn't be able to catch her, for she is as light as the down of a swan. I will put her on a water-lily leaf; it will be just like an island to her. In the meantime, we shall get your house, down in the mud, ready for your marriage."

Out in the stream grew many water lilies, and all of their leaves looked as if they were floating in the water. The biggest of them was the farthest from shore; on that one the old toad put Thumbelina's little bed.

When the poor little girl woke in the morning and saw where she was—on a green leaf with water all around her—she began to cry bitterly. There was no way of getting to shore at all.

The old toad was very busy down in her mud house, decorating the walls with reeds and yellow flowers that grew near the shore. She meant to do her best for her new daughter-in-law. After she had finished, she and her ugly son swam out to the water-lily leaf to fetch Thumbelina's bed. It was to be put in the bridal chamber. The old toad curtsied—and that is not easy to do while you are swimming. Then she said, "Here is my son. He is to be your husband; you two will live happily down in the mud."

"Croak! . . . Croak!" was all the son said. Then they took the bed and swam away with it. Poor Thumbelina sat on the green leaf and wept and wept, for she did not want to live with the ugly toad and have her hideous son as a husband. The little fishes that were swimming around in the brook had heard what the old toad said; they stuck their heads out of the water to take a look at the tiny girl. When they saw how beautiful she was, it hurt them to think that she should have to marry the ugly toad and live in the mud. They decided that they would not let it happen, and gathered around the green stalk that held the leaf anchored to the bottom of the stream. They all nibbled on the stem, and soon the leaf was free. It drifted down the stream, bearing Thumbelina far away from the ugly toad.

As Thumbelina sailed by, the little birds on the shore saw her and sang, "What a lovely little girl." Farther and farther sailed the leaf with its little passenger, taking her on a journey to foreign lands.

For a long time a lovely white butterfly flew around her; then it landed on the leaf. It had taken a fancy to Thumbelina. The tiny girl laughed, for she was happy to have escaped the toad and the stream was so beautiful, golden in the sunshine. She took the little silk ribbon that she wore around her waist and tied one end of it to the butterfly and the other to the water-lily leaf. Now the leaf raced down the stream—and so did Thumbelina, for she was standing on it.

*A*t that moment a big May bug flew by; when it spied Thumbelina, it swooped down and with its claws grabbed the poor girl around her tiny waist and flew up into a tree with her. The leaf floated on down the stream, and the butterfly had to follow it.

Little Thumbelina was terrified as the May bug flew away with her, but stronger than her fear was her grief for the poor little white butterfly that she had chained to the leaf with her ribbon. If he did not get loose, he would starve to death.

The May bug didn't care what happened to the butterfly. He placed Thumbelina on the biggest leaf on the tree. He gave her honey from the flowers to eat, and told her that she was the loveliest thing he had ever seen, even though she didn't look like a May bug. Soon all the other May bugs that lived in the tree came visiting. Two young lady May bugs—they were still unmarried—wiggled their antennae and said: "She has only two legs, how wretched! No antennae and a thin waist, how disgusting! She looks like a human being, how ugly!"

All the other female May bugs agreed with them. The May bug who had caught Thumbelina still thought her lovely; but when all the others kept insisting that she was ugly, he soon was convinced of it too. Now he didn't want her any longer, and put her down on a daisy at the foot of the tree, and told her she could go wherever she wanted to for all he cared. Poor Thumbelina cried; she thought it terrible to be so ugly that even a May bug would not want her, though in truth she was more beautiful than you can imagine, more lovely than the petal of the most beautiful rose.

*A*ll summer long poor Thumbelina lived all alone in the forest. She wove a hammock out of grass and hung it underneath a dock leaf so that it would not rain on her while she slept. She ate the honey in the flowers and drank the dew that was on their leaves every morning.

Summer and autumn passed. But then came winter: the long, cold winter. All the birds that had sung so beautifully flew away. The flowers withered; the trees lost their leaves; and the dock leaf that had protected her rolled itself up and became a shriveled yellow stalk. She was terribly cold. Her clothes were in shreds; and she was so thin and delicate.

Poor Thumbelina; she was bound to freeze to death. It started to snow and each snowflake that fell on her was like a whole shovelful of snow would be to us, because we are so big and she was so small.

She wrapped herself in a wizened leaf, but it gave no warmth and she shivered from the cold.

Not far from the forest was a big field where grain had grown; only a few dry stubbles still rose from the frozen ground, pointing up to the heavens. To Thumbelina these straws were like a forest. Trembling, she wandered through them and came to the entrance of a field mouse's house. There the mouse lived in warmth and comfort, with a full larder and a nice kitchen. Like a beggar child, Thumbelina stood outside the door and begged for a single grain of barley. It had been several days since she had last eaten.

"Poor little wretch," said the field mouse, for she had a kind heart. "Come down into my warm living room and dine with me."

The field mouse liked Thumbelina. "You can stay the winter," she said. "But you must keep the room tidy and tell me a story every day, for I like a good story." Thumbelina did what the kind old mouse demanded, and she lived quite happily.

"Soon we shall have a visitor," said the mouse. "Once a week my neighbor comes. He lives even more comfortably than I do. He has a drawing room, and wears the most exquisite black fur coat. If only he would marry you, then you would be well provided for. He can't see you, for he is blind, so you will have to tell him the very best of your stories."

But Thumbelina did not want to marry the mouse's neighbor, for he was a mole. The next day he came visiting, dressed in his black velvet fur coat. The field mouse said that he was both rich and wise. His house was twenty times as big as hers, and he was cultured too. But he did not like the sun nor the beautiful flowers; he said they were abominable, for he had never seen them. Thumbelina had to sing for him; and when she sang "*Frère Jacques, dormez-vous*?" he fell in love with her because of her beautiful voice; but he didn't show it, for he was sober-minded and never made a spectacle of himself.

He had recently dug a passage from his own house to theirs, and he invited Thumbelina and the field mouse to use it as often as they pleased. He told them not to be afraid of the dead bird in the corridor. It had died only a few days before. It was still whole and had all its feathers. By chance it had been buried in his passageway.

The mole took a piece of dry rotten wood in his mouth; it shone as brightly as fire in the darkness; then he led the way down through the long corridor. When they came to the place where the dead bird lay, the mole made a hole with his broad nose, up through the earth, so that light could come through. Almost blocking the passageway was a dead swallow, with its beautiful wings pressed close to its body, its feet almost hidden by feathers, and its head nestled under a wing. The poor bird undoubtedly had frozen to death. Thumbelina felt a great sadness; she had loved all the birds that twittered and sang for her that summer.

*T*he mole kicked the bird with one of his short legs and said, "Now it has stopped chirping. What a misfortune it is to be born a bird. Thank God, none of my children will be born birds! All they can do is chirp, and then die of starvation when winter comes."

"Yes, that's what all sensible people think," said the field mouse. "What does all that chirping lead to? Starvation and cold when winter comes. But I suppose they think it is romantic."

Thumbelina didn't say anything, but when the mouse and mole had their backs turned, she leaned down and kissed the closed eye of the swallow. "Maybe that was one of the birds that sang so beautifully for me this summer," she thought. "How much joy you gave me, beautiful little bird."

The mole closed the hole through which the daylight had entered and then escorted the ladies home. That night Thumbelina could not sleep; she rose and wove as large a blanket as she could out of hay. She carried it down the dark passage and covered the little bird with it. In the field mouse's living room she had found bits of cotton; she tucked them under the swallow wherever she could, to protect it from the cold earth.

"Good-bye, beautiful bird," she said. "Good-bye, and thank you for the songs you sang for me when it was summer and all the trees were green and the sun warmed us."

She put her head on the bird's breast; then she jumped up! Something was ticking inside: it was the bird's heart, for the swallow was not really dead, and now the warmth had revived it.

In the autumn all the swallows fly to the warm countries. If one tarries too long and is caught by the first frost, he lies down on the ground as if he were dead, and the cold snow covers him.

Thumbelina shook with fear. The swallow was huge to a girl so tiny. But she gathered her courage and pressed the blanket closer to the bird's body. She even went to fetch the little mint leaf that she herself used as a cover and put it over the bird's head.

The next night she sneaked down to the passageway again; the bird was better although still very weak. He opened his eyes just long enough to see Thumbelina standing in the dark with a little piece of dry rotten wood in her hand as a lamp.

"Thank you, you sweet little child," said the sick swallow, "I feel much better. I am not cold now. Soon I shall be strong again and can fly out into the sunshine."

"Oh, no," she said. "It is cold and snowing outside now and you would freeze. Stay down here in your warm bed. I will nurse you."

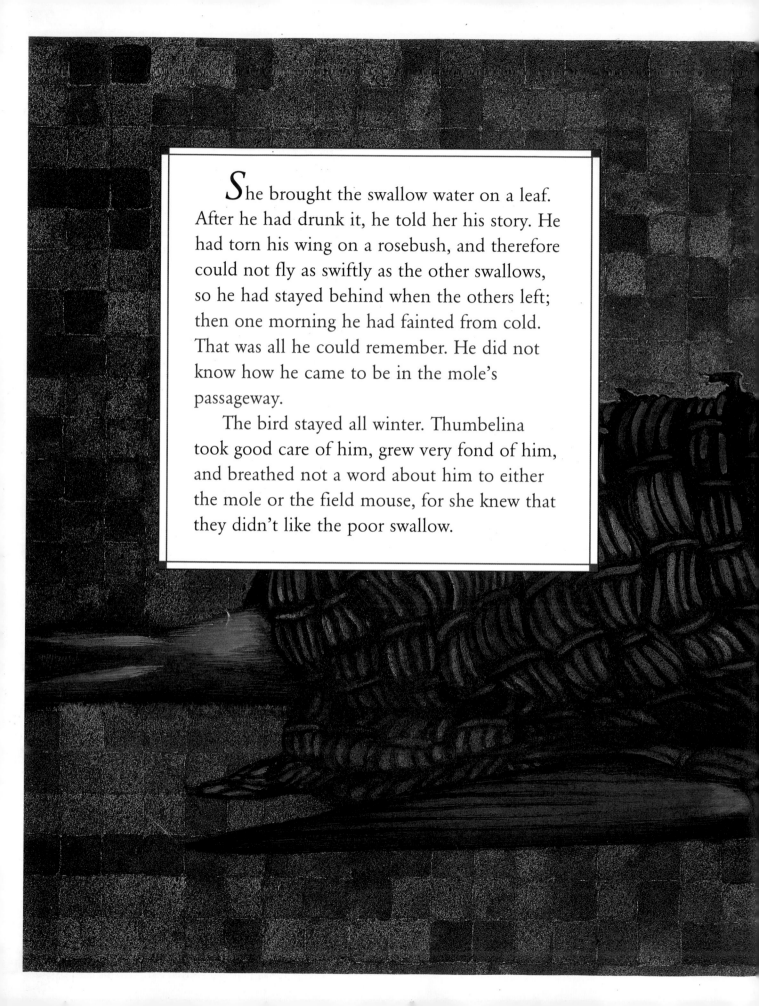

She brought the swallow water on a leaf.
After he had drunk it, he told her his story. He
had torn his wing on a rosebush, and therefore
could not fly as swiftly as the other swallows,
so he had stayed behind when the others left;
then one morning he had fainted from cold.
That was all he could remember. He did not
know how he came to be in the mole's
passageway.

The bird stayed all winter. Thumbelina
took good care of him, grew very fond of him,
and breathed not a word about him to either
the mole or the field mouse, for she knew that
they didn't like the poor swallow.

*A*s soon as spring came and the warmth of the sun could be felt through the earth, the swallow said good-bye to Thumbelina, who opened the hole that the mole had made. The sun shone down pleasantly. The swallow asked her if she did not want to come along with him; she could sit on his back and he would fly with her out into the great forest. But Thumbelina knew that the field mouse would be sad and lonely if she left.

"I cannot," she said.

The bird thanked her once more. "Farewell. . . . Farewell, lovely girl," he sang, and flew out into the sunshine.

Thumbelina's eyes filled with tears as she watched the swallow fly away, for she cared so much for the bird.

"Tweet . . . tweet," he sang, and disappeared in the forest.

Poor Thumbelina was miserable. Soon the grain would be so tall that the field would be in shade, and she would no longer be able to enjoy the warm sunshine.

"This summer you must spend getting your trousseau ready," said the field mouse, for the sober mole in the velvet coat had proposed to her. "You must have both woolens and linen to wear and to use in housekeeping when you become Mrs. Mole."

Thumbelina had to spin by hand and the field mouse hired four spiders to weave both night and day. Every evening the mole came visiting, but all he talked about was how nice it would be when the summer was over. He didn't like the way the sun baked the earth; it made it hard to dig in. As soon as autumn came they would get married. But Thumbelina was not happy; she thought the mole was dull and she did not love him. Every day, at sunrise and at sunset, she tiptoed to the entrance of the field mouse's house, so that when the wind blew and parted the grain, she could see the blue sky above her. She thought of how light and beautiful it was out there, and she longed for her friend the swallow. "He is probably far away in the wonderful green forest!" she thought. "And he will never come back."

*A*utumn came and Thumbelina's trousseau was finished.

"In four weeks we shall hold your wedding," said the field mouse.

Thumbelina cried and said she did not want to marry the boring old mole.

"Fiddlesticks!" squeaked the field mouse. "Don't be stubborn or I will bite you with my white teeth. You are getting an excellent husband; he has a velvet coat so fine that the queen does not have one that is better. He has both a larder and kitchen; you ought to thank God for giving you such a good husband."

The day of the wedding came; the mole had already arrived. Thumbelina grieved. Now she would never see the warm sun again. The mole lived far down under the ground, for he didn't like the sun. While she lived with the field mouse, she at least had been allowed to walk as far as the entrance of the little house and look at the sun.

"Farewell. . . . Farewell, you beautiful sun!" Thumbelina lifted her hands up toward the sky and then took a few steps out upon the field. The harvest was over and only stubbles were left. She saw a little red flower. Embracing it, she said: "Farewell! And give my love to the swallow if you ever see him."

"Tweet . . . Tweet," something said in the air above her.

She looked up. It was the little swallow. As soon as he saw Thumbelina he chirped with joy. And she told the bird how she had to marry the awful mole, and live forever down under the ground, and never see the sun again. The very telling of her future brought tears to her eyes.

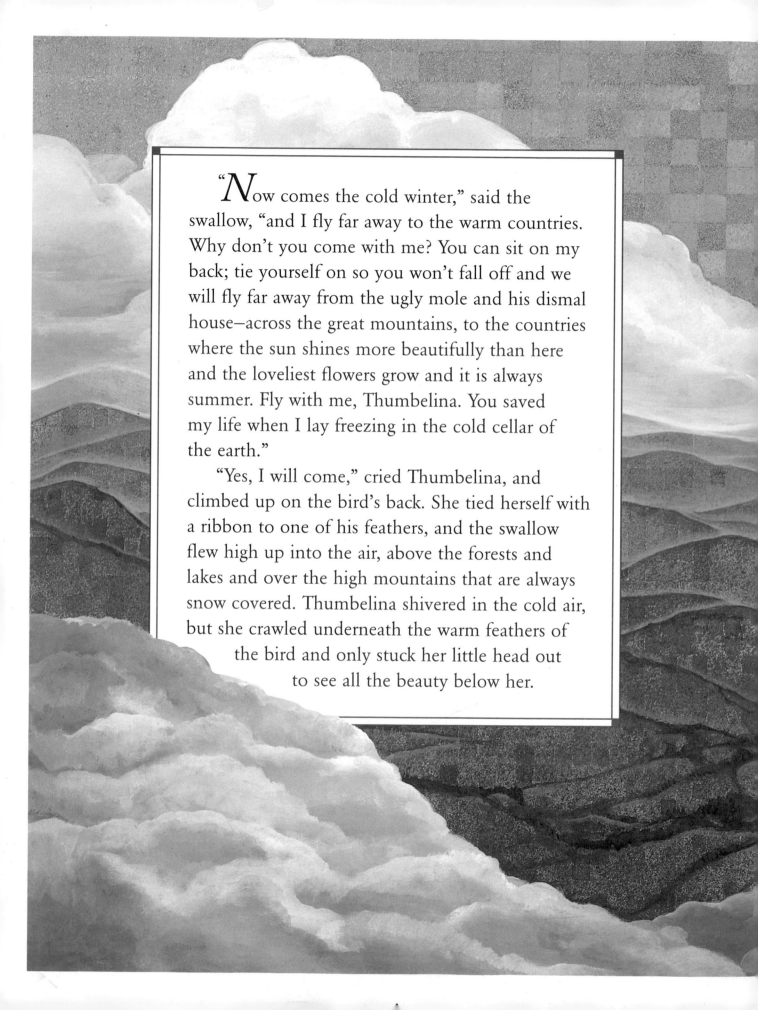

"*N*ow comes the cold winter," said the swallow, "and I fly far away to the warm countries. Why don't you come with me? You can sit on my back; tie yourself on so you won't fall off and we will fly far away from the ugly mole and his dismal house—across the great mountains, to the countries where the sun shines more beautifully than here and the loveliest flowers grow and it is always summer. Fly with me, Thumbelina. You saved my life when I lay freezing in the cold cellar of the earth."

"Yes, I will come," cried Thumbelina, and climbed up on the bird's back. She tied herself with a ribbon to one of his feathers, and the swallow flew high up into the air, above the forests and lakes and over the high mountains that are always snow covered. Thumbelina shivered in the cold air, but she crawled underneath the warm feathers of the bird and only stuck her little head out to see all the beauty below her.

*T*hey came to the warm countries. And what the swallow had said was true: the sun shone more brightly and the sky seemed twice as high. Along the fences grew the loveliest green and blue grapes. From the trees in the forests hung oranges and lemons. Along the roads the most beautiful children ran, chasing many-colored butterflies. The swallow flew even farther south, and the landscape beneath them became more and more beautiful.

Near a forest, on the shores of a lake, stood the ruins of an ancient temple; ivy wound itself around the white pillars. On top of these were many swallows' nests, and one of them belonged to the little swallow that was carrying Thumbelina.

"This is my house," he said. "Now choose for yourself one of the beautiful flowers down below and I will set you down on it. It will make a lovely home for you."

"How wonderful!" exclaimed Thumbelina, and clapped her hands. Among the broken white marble pillars grew tall, lovely, white flowers. The swallow set her down on the leaves of one of them; and to Thumbelina's astonishment, she saw a little man sitting in the center of the flower. He was white and almost transparent, as if he were made of glass. On his head he wore a golden crown. On his back were a pair of wings. He was no taller than Thumbelina. In every one of the flowers there lived such a tiny angel; and this one was the king of them all.

"How handsome he is!" whispered Thumbelina to the swallow.

The tiny little king was terrified of the bird, which was several times larger than he was. But when he saw Thumbelina he forgot his fear. She was the loveliest creature he had ever seen; and so he took the crown off his own head and put it on hers. Then he asked her what her name was and whether she wanted to be queen of the flowers.

Now here was a better husband than old mother toad's ugly son or the mole with the velvet coat. Thumbelina said yes; and from all the flowers came lovely little angels to pay homage to their queen. How lovely and delicate they all were; and they brought her gifts, and the best of these was a pair of wings, so that she would be able to fly, as they all did, from flower to flower.

It was a day of happiness. And the swallow, from his nest in the temple, sang for them as well as he could. But in his heart he was sad, for he, too, loved Thumbelina and had hoped never to be parted from her.

"You shall not be called Thumbelina any longer," said the king. "It is an ugly name. From now on we shall call you Maja."

"Farewell! Farewell!" called the little swallow. He flew back to the north, away from the warm countries. He came to Denmark; and there he has his nest, above the window of a man who can tell fairy tales.

"Tweet . . . tweet," sang the swallow. And the man heard it and wrote down the whole story.